BET 7.11

numbers

a book by John J. Reiss

Bradbury Press • Scarsdale, N.Y.

J
R

Library of Congress Catalog Card Number: 76-151313
Manufactured in the United States of America
ISBN 0-02-776150-9
The typeface used in this book is Helvetica.
The illustrations, composed of forms cut
from colored glazed papers, are reproduced
in full color.

6 7 8 9   83 84 85

To Kenny Brown and Meg Moynihan

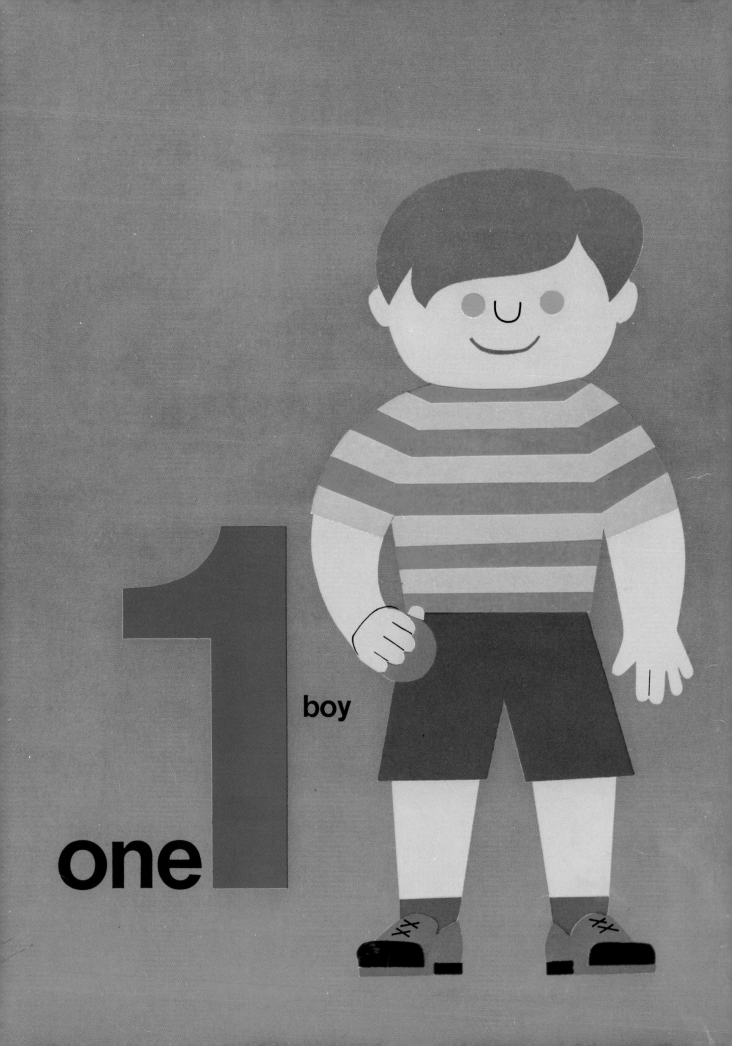

one 1 boy

socks

2

two

shoes

clover leaf

traffic lights

3

three

4

legs

four

wheels

starfish arms

five 5

six **6**

birthday candles

horse-chestnut leaf

7

seven

ravens

eight **8**

reindeer

nine 9

baseball players

houses

ten 10

toes

kites

eleven 11

twelve **12**

hours

cakes

13

thirteen

14
fourteen
bananas

grapefruit

15

fifteen

16
sixteen

pigeons

marbles

17

seventeen

18

eighteen

crayons

radishes

19

nineteen

20

twenty

portholes

thirty **30**

fingers

flowers

forty

40

fifty
50

candy kisses

sixty lollipops

60

70

seventy

beads

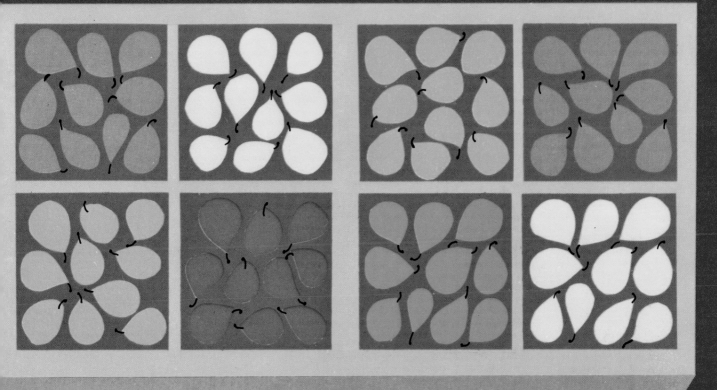

pears

eighty

80

90

ninety

gumballs

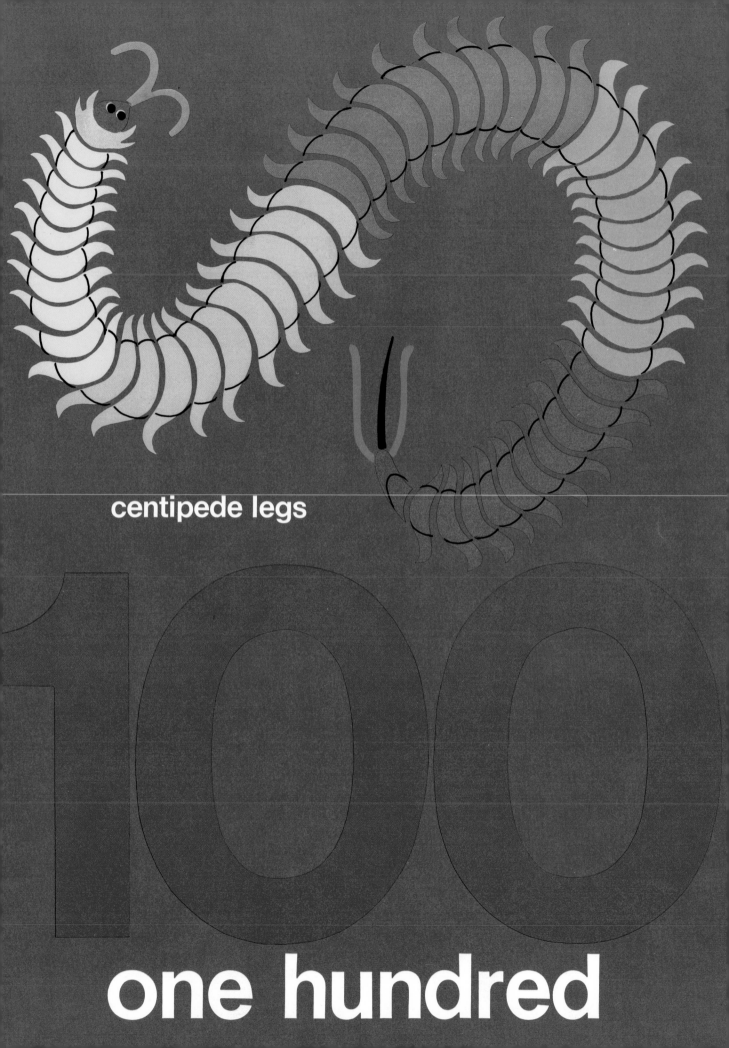

centipede legs

100

one hundred

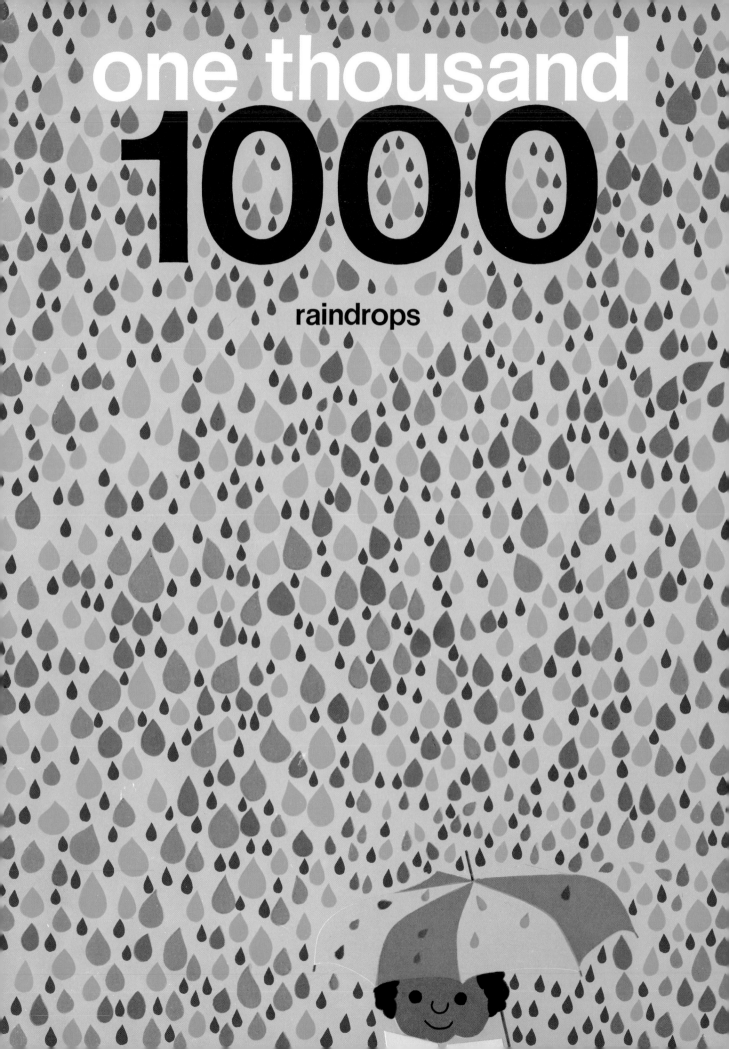

one thousand
1000
raindrops